The Goodbye Walk

by Joanne Ryder/illustrated by Deborah Haeffele

Dutton   **Lodestar Books**   New York

Text copyright © 1993 by Joanne Ryder
Illustrations copyright © 1993 by Deborah Haeffele

Library of Congress Cataloging-in-Publication Data

Ryder, Joanne.

The goodbye walk/by Joanne Ryder; illustrated by Deborah Haeffele.—1st ed.
p. cm.
Summary: At the end of the summer, a child revisits the
special places she has enjoyed on her vacation.
ISBN 0–525–67405–5
[1. Summer—Fiction. 2. Vacations—Fiction.] I. Haeffele, Deborah, ill.   II. Title.
PZ7.R959Go   1993
[E]—dc20
92–10325
CIP
AC

Published in the United States by Lodestar Books,
an affiliate of Dutton Children's Books,
a division of Penguin Books USA Inc.,
375 Hudson Street, New York, New York 10014

Published simultaneously in Canada
by McClelland & Stewart, Toronto

Editor: Virginia Buckley
Designers: Deborah & Steven Haeffele

Printed in Hong Kong
First Edition
10 9 8 7 6 5 4 3 2 1

to Beth Urquhart,
who believed in people and good books
Goodbye
J.R.

to Betty Abel,
my first and best art teacher

D.H.

It takes time
to get to know
a special place,
time to explore
new paths
and see new things.
And then one day
it's time to
say goodbye.

When you take
a goodbye walk,
you know
just where
you want to go,
which paths
will lead you there.

Along your way
are landmarks
you remember:
a row of tall pines
pointing to the sky,
a shady wall of ferns . . .

And an old sign
leaning toward the sea.
You smile
and watch
your landmarks
passing by
as you walk
past them
one more time.

You are busy
on a goodbye walk
looking here and there,
gathering memories
as you go.
You see things
as they are today,
and also
as they were
on other days
when summer
was long and new.

Then a flag-tailed dog
ran up the hill,
leaping high to greet you.
A thousand berries
tinged the bushes black,
and you stopped
to eat them
sun-warmed and sweet.

Today
someone may wave,
glad to see you.
You pause
to say goodbye,
to play a game,
to run together
one last time
through grass
grown thick and tall.

On a goodbye walk
you can stop
as you please—
on the bridge
where young fish
hide below,
waiting for you
and your bread .   .   .

on the hill
where eagles
soar above you
like dark kites
without strings . . .
on the pebbly beach
where a cool wind
catches you at last.
You wrap
yourself up
and feel summer
blowing away.

On a goodbye walk
you may even see
something new,
someone you
have never seen before.
Bend down and greet
a sea star glowing brightly
in a rocky pool,
a bold crab
creeping sideways,
its claws stretched wide
to fight your shadow
dancing on the water.

Gaze out and greet
a tall bird standing still,
hunting for fish
an island away.
Meeting someone new
makes you smile.
And you say,
"Hello,"
not "Goodbye."

Somewhere
along your path
a secret place
you know by heart
will call you.
Your feet follow footsteps
you've made before
to a cave snug and dry
at the edge of the sea.
Water, calm and blue,
sparkles and dances,
sliding closer to you
as the tide rises
touching rocks and sand.
This place is
as good as the first
time you saw it.
Even better.

And when
it's time to leave,
you call, "Goodbye."
You wish
this spot well
and hope
you'll return one day
to find it
just as special
as it is today.

On the way back
you run down the hill
and feel the world
tilting beneath you again.

You wade
through the stream
that once tickled your knees
and now tickles your ankles
as you splash,
a cool fish in the sun.
You pick
the last berries,
tasting them
and this day
as sweet as
all the rest.

At the end
of a goodbye walk
your arms
may be empty,
but you are full
of things
to take
with you—
feelings
and sights
tucked deep
inside you,

memories
to keep
forever
and ever.